AgriKids makes it fun for children to learn about farm safety and discover all there is to love about rural life.

To learn more about our products and what we do, visit AgriKids.ie.

For my farmer, Mark, and
future farmer, Eamon.
Stay safe!

TALES FROM RIVERSIDE FARM

THE TREE SWING

ALMA JORDAN

ILLUSTRATED BY
MARTIN BECKETT

AgriKids
BE FARM SAFE
STAY FARM
SAFE

First published in 2015 by
AgriKids
Ashbawn, Corbal-lis,
Julianstown, Co. Meath
www.agrikids.ie

Paperback	ISBN: 978 1 909483 86 6
eBook – mobi format	ISBN: 978 1 909483 87 3
eBook – ePub format	ISBN: 978 1 909483 88 0
CreateSpace edition	ISBN: 978 1 909483 89 7

Produced by Kazoo Independent Publishing Services
222 Beech Park, Lucan, Co. Dublin
www.kazoopublishing.com

Kazoo Independent Publishing Services is not the publisher of this work. All rights and responsibilities pertaining to this work remain with AgriKids.

Kazoo offers independent authors a full range of publishing services.
For further details visit www.kazoopublishing.com

Cover design by Andrew Brown
Cover and internal illustrations © Martin Beckett, One Tree Studio Ltd
Printed in the EU

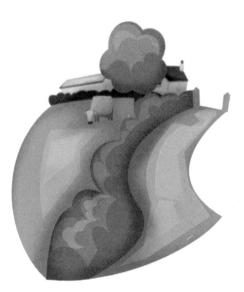

Down a twisty lane near the village of Ballymalley, you will find Riverside Farm.

Tom and Sarah live on the
farm with Mammy, Daddy
and Meg, their sheepdog.

They have hens, horses, sheep,
cows and some
very NOISY
GEESE.

Of all the animals, Tom
and Sarah love the chickens
the most.

They collect the eggs every day after school and eat them for their breakfast the next morning.

There is always lots of work to do at Riverside Farm.

The baby lambs are born in spring, and in summer it's time to make the hay.

Autumn is harvest
time, and in winter
Daddy ploughs
the fields.

Now it was
summer and the school
holidays had just begun. It was
a beautiful day at Riverside
Farm.

'I'M BORED!' said Tom.

'ME TOO,' said Sarah.

'I have an idea,' said Mammy. 'Why don't you go camping in the garden? If it doesn't rain, you can sleep out there tonight.'

Tom and Sarah loved this idea, and they ran to the garden shed to find their TENT.

It was hard work, but soon the
tent was ready,
although it
looked a bit
WOBBLY in
places!

'I hope it doesn't FALL DOWN,'
said Sarah.

'Don't worry,' said Tom, 'it will
be fine.'

That night they snuggled into their sleeping bags.

 Meg was lying beside them, watching them eat peanut butter sandwiches and drink hot chocolate.

'Mmmm, sandwiches taste
much better outside,' said
Sarah.

'WOOF!'

Meg's bark gave them both a fright.

'What's wrong, Meg?' asked Tom. 'Is there something OUTSIDE?'

Meg SNIFFED the air.

'Dogs can smell things that you and I can't,' said Sarah. 'I think Meg smelled something STRANGE.'

'GRRRRRR!' Meg growled.

Sarah jumped up. 'I'm going out to see,' she said.

'NO, Sarah!' whispered Tom. 'We should stay inside.'

'Don't be such a SCAREDY CAT,' said Sarah. 'It's probably just Mrs Kelly's cat hunting for mice.'

Sarah zipped open the tent.
Meg dashed out and
jumped up and down
at the garden hedge.

Then they heard a
little voice. It was coming from
inside the hedge.

'HELP! OH, PLEASE HELP!'

Sarah looked at Tom and put her finger to her lips.

 'SHHHH! I think someone is in our hedge,' she whispered.

'Please HELP me!' the little voice cried again. 'I'm SCARED of dogs.'

Tom threw his sandwich and
Meg ran after it.

She was excited to get some
yummy peanut butter.

21

'Hello,' said Tom. 'It's safe to come out now.'

'Is the DOG gone?' said the little voice.

'YES,' said the children.

The hedge began to glow, BRIGHTER and BRIGHTER. It got so bright that the children had to cover their eyes.

When they opened them
again, they saw something
very strange – a TINY creature,
 no bigger than a tin of
BEANS, with curly red
hair and a little TOP HAT.

He was able to fly thanks
to his huge ears, which
FLUTTERED like butterfly wings.
Tom and Sarah gasped.

'W-W-WHO are you?' asked
Tom.

The little creature smiled, lifted
 his hat from his
head and said,
'How do you
do? I'm Mr
Brambles.'

'Are you a FAIRY?' asked Tom.

'A FAIRY!' said Mr Brambles. 'I am nothing like a fairy!'

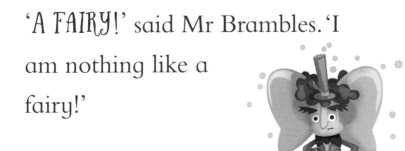

'Fairies are only good at collecting old teeth and being very bossy,' he said.

'I am a HEDGE SPRITE and our work is far more important than fairy work.'

'A HEDGE SPRITE?' said Sarah. 'There's no such thing.'

'I beg your pardon,' said Mr Brambles. 'Hedge sprites are as real as butterflies and earthworms.'

'Really?' said Sarah. 'Can you do MAGIC?'

'Of course,' said Mr Brambles. 'Hedge sprites make the flowers smell wonderful!'

'IMPOSSIBLE!' said Sarah. 'I don't believe you.'

'Don't be so rude, Sarah,' said Tom. 'How do you make all those smells, Mr Brambles?'

'The ingredients are all around us,' said Mr Brambles.

'Two drops of morning dew, one drop of summer rain or a pinch of a BLACKBIRD'S song.'

'Sometimes I add a swish of a summer breeze or a ladybird's sneeze. Then a tap or two of my magic twig, and PIFF PUFF POOF, you have the perfect pong!'

The children were AMAZED.
This was important work
indeed.

'I'm sorry I was rude, Mr
Brambles. My name is Sarah
and this is Tom. Would you
like to share some hot
chocolate?'

'MMMMMM, delicious!' Mr Brambles slurped his creamy hot chocolate.

'Thank you for SAVING ME. I don't like DOGS very much, or CATS.'

'Meg is a friendly dog,' said Sarah.

Meg trotted over to Mr
Brambles and gave him a big
sloppy lick.

'YUCK, I'm soaked,' he said, but
he was laughing too.

'I must be getting HOME. It's getting late, and Mrs Brambles will be worried,' said Mr Brambles.

'But before I go, I would like to repay you for your KINDNESS, so remember this: Should you ever be in FEAR, call THREE TIMES and I will hear.'

Mr Brambles fluttered his ears, floated above their heads and in a FLASH he was gone.

The children were so excited after meeting their new friend that they didn't sleep a WINK.

The next morning, after GOBBLING up their breakfast, 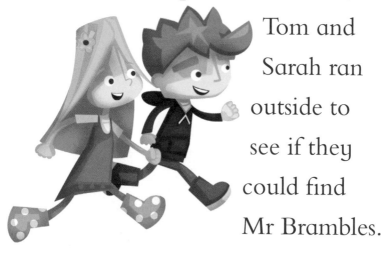 Tom and Sarah ran outside to see if they could find Mr Brambles.

But he was NOWHERE to be seen.

'Maybe he's on the farm collecting more perfume potions for the flowers,' said Tom.

'YUCK!' said Sarah. 'I don't think there are any nice smells on the farm.'

Tom and Sarah weren't allowed go to the farm on their own, but they really wanted to find Mr Brambles.

'Let's just have a quick look,' said Tom. 'Mammy and Daddy will never know.'

Daddy and Jack
the farmhand were
cleaning out the cattle shed.

'YUCK!' said Sarah, holding her nose. 'That stinks.'

'Of course it does,' said Tom. 'It's cow POO! Now stay quiet. We don't want them to hear us. We'll be in BIG TROUBLE if we get caught.'

They ran to the paddock.
Maybe their little friend would
be there.

But instead of Mr Brambles,
the children found SOMETHING
ELSE.

'THE TREE SWING!' they both shouted.

The tree swing was a big OLD tyre attached to a tree with some rope.

It had been there a very long time, and the rope was ROTTEN and TATTY.

The children had been told NEVER to play on it.

'I don't think we should be here,' said Sarah.

But Tom wasn't listening. He was too busy climbing through the tyre.

He pushed himself forward as hard as he could. 'Weeeeeee!' he shouted. 'Look, I'm flying!'

Backwards and forwards he swung, higher and higher.

'Look, Sarah, look!' he called.

CREAK,

CREAK,

CREAK went the rope.

The noise grew louder as Tom swung higher and higher, faster and faster.

'Slow down, Tom,' shouted Sarah.

Tom was going really high now, and the butterflies in his tummy made him want to go even higher.

CREAK, creak, creak.

Higher and HIGHER.

CREAK, creak, creak.

Faster and FASTER.

'Tom, please SLOW DOWN,' Sarah cried.

Then she remembered what Mr Brambles had told them: 'Should you ever be in FEAR, call THREE TIMES and I will hear.'

 'Mr Brambles, Mr Brambles, Mr Brambles,' called Sarah.

But it was too late. Suddenly the rope snapped and Tom and the tyre came crashing towards the ground.

'Tom!' shouted Sarah as her brother fell.

WHOOOOOOOSH!

There was a bright
flash, and then
Tom wasn't
falling any more.

Instead he was floating in the air. It was magic – hedge sprite magic!

Very, very slowly, Tom landed softly on the grass. He was as white as a ghost!

Mr Brambles appeared beside
Tom as he got to his feet. 'Are
you OK, Tom?' he asked.

'You are a very LUCKY boy. Thank goodness Sarah remembered what to do.'

'Thanks, Sarah,' Tom said, feeling a little SILLY. 'And THANK YOU, Mr Brambles.'

They all turned around when they heard a VOICE.

'Tom and Sarah, what are you up to?'

It was Daddy, and he was RUNNING towards them.

'He must have heard me SHOUTING,' said Sarah.

'OH DEAR,' said Mr Brambles. 'I mustn't let a grown-up see me.'

'Goodbye, children and
remember to be more CAREFUL
in future. SWINGS and things
are only for PLAYGROUNDS and
BACK GARDENS, where your
mammy or daddy can see
you.'

Daddy was very CROSS with Tom and Sarah. 'I told you before not to use the old SWING,' he said. 'You could have been badly HURT, Tom.'

'SORRY, Daddy,' said Tom.

'I should have taken it down ages ago,' said Daddy. 'You two are never to come to the farm alone again. Do you understand?'

'YES,' the children said quietly.

NOW they were both very sorry.

Later that day, Daddy took down the tyre swing and put it with all the other tyres on the silage pit.

Meanwhile, in the hedge at the back of the garden, Mr Brambles told Mrs Brambles all about his afternoon.

'WELL DONE, Mr Brambles,' she said, and she gave him a big kiss.

'I hope Tom and Sarah have learned their lesson,' he said. 'FARMS can be dangerous places.'

Not too long after, Mr Brambles heard laughter coming from Tom and Sarah's back garden.

He poked his head through the hedge and gasped with DELIGHT.

The children were playing on
a brand-new set of SWINGS.

There was a climbing wall,
two swings and even a tree
house.

'HIGHER, Daddy, higher,' Sarah shouted.

'No, that's high enough,' said Daddy.

'WEEEEEE!' said Tom, coming down the slide.

What a happy sight it was.

That night as he lay tucked up in his bed, Mr Brambles knew there would be no more tree swings at Riverside Farm ever again.